The Powers That Be

AMY LAURENS

OTHER WORKS

SANCTUARY SERIES

Where Shadows Rise
Through Roads Between
When Worlds Collide

KADITEOS SERIES

How Not To Acquire A Castle
Define Good (2020)
How Not To Ring The Hero's Bell (2020)

STORM FOXES SERIES

A Fox of Storms and Starlight

SHORT WORKS

Darkness and Good
Dreaming Of Forests
Of Sea Foam and Blood

NON-FICTION

How To Write Dogs
How To Theme
How To Create Cultures
How To Create Life
How To Map
The 32 Worst Mistakes People Make About Dogs

Find other works by the author at
www.amylaurens.com

The Powers That Be

INKLET #26

AMY LAURENS

www.inkprintpress.com

Print ISBN: 978-1-925825-31-2
eBook ISBN: 9781393830740

www.inkprintpress.com

National Library of Australia Cataloguing-in-Publication Data
Laurens, Amy 1985 –
The Powers That Be
84 p.
ISBN: 978-1-925825-31-2
Inkprint Press, Canberra, Australia
1. Fiction—Superheroes 2. Fiction—Fantasy—Urban 3.
Fiction—Romance—Fantasy 4. Fiction— Short Stories

First Print Edition: January 2020
Cover image © Inarik via Deposit Photos
Cover design © Inkprint Press
Interior art © Amy Laurens

THE POWERS THAT BE

Rordan stood watching in the frosty street as the last Power, a man with eyes too old for his ancient body, was escorted through double steel doors that mirrored the coal-dusted snow of the footpath.

A doctor paused to address the crowd: the last of the Powers secured, found holed up in an old weatherboard lean-to in the railyards, old and frail, wasting away. He'd forgotten who he was, the doctor said. Lost himself in a fog of age and mental decline. But they had him now, and he was safe, and soon the world would be too.

And although Rordan held his head high and cheered with the rest of the crowd, he couldn't pretend his chest didn't writhe with anguish.

When Hunger had been defeated, Rordan had cheered along with everybody else and meant it. It seemed right and natural that Plenty should conquer. And no one had been disappointed when the twin powers of Pestilence and Pollution had followed; Purity was quite obviously a preferable ruler.

Even earlier that than, a decade again, right at the beginning, Peace had made an open bid for leadership, becoming the first Power in recorded history to be elected to an official human government—but it got Rordan to wondering: Peace had only seemed to triumph in the absence of War by teaming up with Innocence, an alliance itself only made possible by the capture of the golden-eyed Power called Understanding during Peace's election campaign—and Rordan had felt like he was the only one to think that maybe Innocence had another, second name that also began with 'i' but was much, much uglier.

And then Innocence, too, had 'disappeared,' and riots began in every major city up and down the east coast as fear spread through the human population like lightning.

Rordan had covered some of the early skirmishes, and the stink of burnt-out storefronts skulking like death in the snowy streets, the way the wind shook the ash from blackened wall studs to powder down like transposed snowflakes, the way the acrid remains of melted plastic set his eyes watering and caught in the back of his throat... He wouldn't forget that. Not as long as he lived.

Peace had been short-lived after that, the first official casualty of the campaign to rid the world of Powers, and it had spiralled down from there. Hundreds of scapegoats had been murdered as passionate lynch-mobs raged, until the government had stepped in with its formal Powers Removal Act.

Everyone had cheered. The world would be safer now.

But they missed the fundamental point, Rordan felt. He reached into his coat pocket for a cigarette and lit it, a small glow of warmth to fight the freeze of winter.

You needed a War to remind you the value of Peace—and to keep Peace accountable for the methods he chose to employ. Now there was no one, and no accountability at all.

Rordan sighed.

In front of him, a girl turned: a pretty girl, with eyes of flame and hair of burnished copper.

Something about that description made him look again, but no; she was just an ordinary girl, with brown eyes, brown hair, average height, average build.

Average. That's what the world was condemned to be, now that the Powers had all gone forever. Ordinary.

Sometimes, he felt like everyone else forgot that *ordinary* was just a synonym for *mediocre*.

The crowd jostled him, and he shrugged away.

What good was it, standing here, anyway? He'd got the story, seen them cart old Simon into the 'farewell wing', hands cuffed behind his back and eyes covered with the now-traditional pitch-black cloth.

Silver eyes, if Rordan remembered correctly, which was more difficult these days. The silver sheen of age and wisdom, so appropriate for the Power whose name was Memory.

And now he'd heard the hospital's official statement, and all the loose ends were tied up. Yes. He stomped his feet to wake them in the cold, and turned up the collar of his fawn-coloured overcoat. He had his story. Time to leave.

He tossed his cigarette into the slurried snow, not bothering to put it out—the trampling feet of the on-lookers would do that well enough.

He didn't see the average woman turn and watch him go; nor did he see her pick up his cigarette butt, blow on it gently to keep it alight, and cradle it in her hands. If he had, it probably wouldn't have made a difference.

She was a Power, after all.

She stared at the ember, glowing softly in her hand, and wondered. Who was he, this stranger who saw through her disguise? What did he want? And, most importantly, how could she use him?

He was too good to waste in the usual way she disposed of men; a bar-room brawl was pointless, even a battle to win her favour too limited in scope.

No. He was special. A man who could see through a Power's disguise could change the world, if she steered him right.

She pocketed the ember and turned back to the doors through which the last security guards were disappearing.

Old Baker boy had been tamed at last. The other man was a puzzle for another time. Today, as Memory died, she was celebrating.

The argument broke out when Rordan arrived back at work, stimulated by his bounty of fresh news.

"Well," said his boss, Jimmy, leaning back in one of the creaky old plastic chairs in the break room, arms folded behind his balding head. "I think they were all a load of hoaxes anyway."

Jane lifted her kitten-covered coffee mug, rolling her blue eyes. "You would. Last time you left this office they didn't have the internet."

"Still don't," Jimmy said, grinning. "Not at home. 'S why I'm here."

Rordan rolled his shoulders uncomfortably, wishing he could say what he felt.

Jimmy, you're a small-minded idiot. Jimmy, you're a bigot and a bastard.

Instead, he unloaded the doughnuts he'd bought from their paper bag, instantly defusing the tension.

Rordan stood by his boss and co-workers, fingers sticky, their mouths full of smooth fat and sweet sugar, and he wondered.

Why *had* the Powers gone? Why *really*? After ruling for hundreds of years, why should they give up their claim to Earth so easily, all at once, to be captured and slowly put to death?

Mental decline. Ha. No. That was what the doctors *wanted* people to think.

Rordan knew better. He licked pink sprinkles from his fingers. "Are they really gone, though, do you think?"

The chatter died around the room as everyone turned to see what would happen.

Jimmy stretched languidly to his feet. "What are you saying?"

Rordan shrugged. "Nothing, really. It just seems all too easy. Convenient. I was wondering, is all."

"Well, you just keep your wonderings to yourself, and write the story you were damn well paid to write. No one wants your conspiracy theories." Jimmy glowered. "Those Powers are gone and we're all going to sleep easier because of it. Damn fool boy, you want people to be scared out of their wits?"

Rordan held up his hands. "I'm sorry! I know what I'm writing, it's fine."

Jimmy snatched up the last doughnut and crammed half of it in his mouth. "Then stick to it." Doughnut crumbs sprayed his shirt. "You aren't paid to think."

Rordan smiled deferentially, and Jimmy turned away. Within moments, conversations had returned to normal and he was free to slip away to his office.

Rordan sat in his narrow office with his back to the tiny, narrow window, ankles crossed, shoulders hunched, pencil tap-tap-tapping on the white Laminex desk like a metronome.

Why had they gone?

Where had they gone?

Twelve Powers, stolen from the world, with no expectation that there would ever be any more after centuries and centuries of their guidance. And all anyone could talk about was how much better it would be without them. Did no one realise how bloody *ordinary* life was without the Powers there to guide? Did no one care?

And how many people had died in the name of ridding the world of Powers? Now they were actually all gone, people had skipped straight to congratulating themselves—as though their pitiful mobs and brainless plans could ever have done anything against Powers who ruled the world. As if humanity could actually have had anything to do with the Powers' disappearance.

Ordinary. And he didn't know why.

Rordan stood suddenly and paced to the tall, narrow window, looking down twenty storeys to the street below, pursing his lips as the coal-stained people hustled on with their lives, hailing coal-stained cabs and crossing coal-stained roads.

Maybe no one *wanted* to know. Maybe like ants, they just wanted to do the job they were paid to do and move on, nothing else to see here, nothing confronting to think about, move along, there's a good chap.

The pencil snapped.

Maybe others didn't care. But he did.

<hr>

She stared up in the slush-covered street at the glass-wrapped high rise, and tapped a warm finger to the tip of her icy chin.

Somewhere, up there, was the man who saw her. She could feel his presence tugging at her like an itch she longed to scratch. She should call in, report to her boss…

But first, she should probably confirm what this new man knew. That'd be the first thing the Boss would want to know anyway.

Someone bumped into her back, and she snickered as a tiny flow of energy left her.

A man raised his voice. "Hey, watch it!"

"I didn't do anything. You watch it!" said another.

Jaw working to hide her grin, she left the two men arguing, heart lifting as one threw his shiny, black briefcase to the ground and waved his fists.

Ah, anger. So sweet.

She entered the high rise through glass double doors, and it was too simple a matter to let the guards argue over whether or not they should let her in while she simply strolled past into the elevator. Far, far too simple, now that the white-eyed coward had gone to his rest and the silver-eyed spoilsport had nearly followed.

Instinct told her she wanted floor thirteen, and after a short, smooth ride, the silver elevator doors shushed open, and she strode easily down the corridors towards the man.

She knew he was there, knew that someone who could see her might undo everything—but she went to him regardless, because people she couldn't control had always fascinated her.

She'd only met three of them before, after all.

She knew who she was, and she had nothing to fear. At the end of a narrow hallway with worn grey carpet, she raised a fist and knocked on a white-painted door.

Rordan jumped away from the window as though looking out it was illegal, tugged his shirt straighter, and crossed to the door. "Don't worry, Jimmy, I'm—"

It was her: the average girl from the street. Average height, average build, eyes of flame and copper hair. He blinked. No, *brown* hair. Brown eyes, brown hair. Plainly brown, plain as the nose on his face.

"Can I help you?" he asked in polite confusion as the hard angle of the door handle dug into his palm.

She smiled a smile that could start wars. "I'm not sure," she said. "I hope so."

She closed the door behind her with a quiet click and frowned, shoving down a lingering twinge of concern.

He was nothing, nobody; he'd been easy as love to sweet-talk; it was nothing but a coincidence after all. She strode through the office, wondering whether to mention the man to her boss. But surely not; he was nothing. No one ever *really* saw her. She'd lived with that so long, she wasn't even sure it was *possible* for someone to see her, now.

She passed into the current floor's reception and rolled her eyes as the rake of a man who thought he was in charge leapt to his feet, hastily tucking in his shirt. Immediately behind him, the secretary straightened in her chair, giggling and re-doing her top button.

Raising an eyebrow, she nodded back the way she'd come. "You're not the only one slacking off. I'd check on the fellow at the end of the corridor if I were you."

The boss-man's livid face as he sputtered protests was payment enough, and she sniggered as she entered the lift. She pulled out her cell phone, flicked it open, and let speed-dial do its thing.

"Yes?" The voice that answered was deep and although it was the sound of a cold wind over a bare hilltop under a velvet midnight sky, the shivers it sent down her spine weren't all bad.

"Good news, boss." Her own voice carried a confidence she never felt around the dark, alluring woman that she now deferred to.

"Mm?"

"It's done. He's gone."

"Perhaps." She could almost see the woman's nostrils flare in restrained disbelief. "I'll not be sure of it until I see it. He has eluded me so many times before."

Well, if anyone knew what Baker was capable of, it was his opposite. "Yes ma'am." She waited as the doors shushed open then crossed the marbled foyer, heels clicking on the black and white slabs.

"Very well," the woman on the phone said at last. "Meet me at the Stag and Pearl. There are things we must... discuss."

The doorman watched the brown-haired woman hang up her phone with a smile that reminded him of the other woman in the nightclub last night, the woman Mickey had stolen right out from underneath his nose. Mickey, who already *had* a girlfriend. Bastard. Mickey, he decided, needed a talking to, something to remind him just exactly who he was dealing with.

The obviously brown-haired woman tossed her hair over her shoulder and laughed as she left the building. What did one man matter, when she could control the rest of them so easily?

Rordan closed the door, slightly confused about the conversation that had just taken place. She'd been charming, brilliant, dazzling, and... And that was just it: and what? He scratched at his temple, clutched at his forehead, trying to retain the memory of the conversation as it began to slip dream-like away.

He found himself staring at the street below, a world of white snow and black soot, so clear-cut, so simple.

He sniffed. If only.

Someone hammered at the door for a brief second before it burst open under the strain. He turned to face Jimmy, who stood in the doorway, red-faced and horrible, pointy little nose making Rordan think for no good reason of a constipated rhinoceros.

Jimmy's jaw worked and his hands fisted and relaxed. "I need that story in half an hour," he said. "Half an hour, you hear?"

Hell, the story. Rordan's stomach dropped even as he nodded. "Sure thing, boss," he said, trying to sound confident. "No problem."

Jimmy left.

He threw one final glance at the window and its black-and-white vista, grabbed his scarf and hat from behind his door, and hurried out. Jimmy would forgive him if the story was late, and he'd never find the story he needed here in the sterility of his steel and glass office.

He needed answers.

<hr>

He wandered through the streets, insubstantial as mist, with no real idea what he was looking for or why. He *had* his story: Simon Baker, last of the Powers at large, Memory, taken away forever to die and be forgotten.

He glanced up at the pearlescent sky. It blinded him with ordinariness. No more flickering lights, no crashes as of thunder as the Powers raged eternal; no more conflict; no more balance.

He scuffed his shoe on the cobbles in frustration. That, there, was the key somehow. Balance; the Powers held the balance of life, and they had for countless millennia. Who would want to change that? Who would dare?

His first thought was of the public figures of the campaign, Alan Ackerman and Binyana Haramis. Gorgeous, charismatic idiots, the pair of them. They didn't have enough cunning to engineer an apple corer, let alone something as deeply complex and political—not to mention dangerous—as the destruction of the Powers. He had that sneaking feeling again, like he was half remembering something important he'd forgotten—or that he was remembering once knowing something important, without knowing what it was.

Rordan tilted his head as a laugh caught his attention. It wound through the crowd, golden and warm, like a host of poppies bobbing in the breeze. Why did that voice, out of all the voices in the crowd, sound familiar?

He should shake it off. He should shrug, and keep walking. He knew that.

But he also knew that he was looking not for *a* story, but for *the* story, and this seemed like a promising start.

She flipped her hair over one shoulder and placed her palm against the door of the bar. Quashing a momentary pang of nerves, she shoved the door open and walked in, stopping just inside in a pose designed to simultaneously invite and incite, and scanned the room. There in the back corner, the place the crowd miraculously seemed to avoid, a dark woman sat at a table in silence.

She flipped her hair again and strutted towards her.

"Can't help yourself, can you?" said the dark woman as she drew close, nodding at the room.

She threw a quick glance backwards, smiling impishly at the chaos. Then she raised an eyebrow at the obvious space around the table. "Neither can you," she replied.

The dark woman pursed her lips, but said nothing further.

She sat. "Are the others coming?"

The dark woman inclined her head towards the door, and she twisted around in her seat to see the twins and a young man filter in. They eased their way between the tables to where the two women sat at the back of the room and pulled out chairs that scraped along the floor with tortured wails so they could join them.

The dark woman nodded curtly and stretched her arms over her head, an apparently casual gesture.

But the lights around them dimmed and the noises of the crowd grew faint, and the red-haired one knew that their table would appear just as insubstantial to the rest of the world.

She held her breath, once again in awe of this woman, this Power, whose powers controlled that which more people feared than anything else: Death.

"So. It begins." Death, voice like the cold night wind, steepled her fingers and gazed at them. "Are you ready?"

The twins nodded without hesitation, followed by the young man. Death turned to the red-haired one and waited.

She fidgeted for a moment, thinking. This was what they had been planning for years; orchestrating the downfall of the well-known Powers had taken decades of careful planning and faked deaths of their own. She should be elated that they were so close to the end. And yet...

And yet. That man had seen her.

But he was only a man. What, really, could he do? And who needed to be seen when they could rule the entire world unfettered? So she met Death's gaze unwaveringly. "Yes. I'm ready."

"Good." Death braided her fingers into a single fist. "The marions have the public convinced that Baker was the last of the Powers, and now that he is out of the way, I can affirm this to people as they sleep. Right now, the world suspects nothing. It is vital that, until the final pieces are in place, we do nothing to arouse suspicion. That means you," she said, peering now with disapproval at the red-haired woman, "must keep yourself under control."

She squirmed in her seat, conscious of the others' eyes on her. "I can do it, don't worry."

Death lifted an eyebrow in the direction of the room at large.

The red-haired woman sighed and leaned forward, pressing her face on the cool laminate of the table. "Fine," she mumbled. "I'm under control."

"No more fights, tiffs, disagreements, arguments?"

Her stomach flipped. Not even disagreements? Did Death know what she was asking, here? "Yes. I promise."

"Good. Then sit up and stop making a spectacle of yourself. There will be plenty of time later for..." She paused to smile dangerously. "Indulgence."

Clunk.

The last five Powers swung around to the noise, unnaturally loud against the cloaking that dulled the room. A man, mouth frozen open in shock and horror, one hand clasping awkwardly at the mug that had fallen.

Not *a* man; *the* man. "He can see us," the red-haired one said quietly.

"Not for long." Death stood, flexing her fingers, dark eyes alight with purpose.

"No, wait." She clutched at Death's arm as she had never dared do before, and likely would never dare do again.

Death glanced at her, eyebrow arched, and she let go her grip—

But it was enough. The man's senses had found him, and he had fled. Death turned to the young man at the table. "Find him."

He stood, nodded, and made his way to the door.

The red-haired woman stormed down the street, fuming. Why had she done that, grabbed Death's arm and let the man escape? He was nothing, less than nothing, just like the rest of these human scum. She lashed out at a crushed Coke can and sent it skittering down the pavement.

A suited man sidestepped it, distaste wrinkling his upper lip, and she snarled at him, bursting with fury, longing to take it out on someone else—but she had promised. That made her snarl again, and she continued down the street with her teeth bared and fists clenched.

What made Death the ruler over all, anyway? Nothing but that the humans feared her most, like they would never fear hunger or plague or the long, slow disaster of the environment, or even war, whose primary purpose at times seemed to be nothing more than homage to Death. All these things were the precursor to Death, but no one ever stopped to consider that. Death *had* no power except that brought to her feet by 'lesser' Powers—she snarled again at that—but no one had ever seemed to realise.

A hunted cry sprang from an alleyway to her right. Her heart leapt. The man.

She burst around the corner of the alleyway, the pounding of her heart telling her that it was too late, too little.

The young man who'd shared a table with her raised his fist—not for the first time, the evidence declared—and the man who could see her flinched, crying out again. The young man punched the other, a good, solid punch that would have rocked anyone on their heels, even if it hadn't been accompanied by a flood of oily-slick darkness and the smell of burnt plastic, decay, and filth.

The man who could see sagged to the ground.

"Stop!" she cried out, voice hoarse, and the young man who was, of course, a Power, turned questioningly to her. "Stop," she tried again, taking the tremor of desperation away and replacing it with command.

She'd never tried to halt a fight before, though technically she could do it. She watched the Power's eyes for signs he might disobey her, coiled tight like a snake about to strike—but the fight ebbed from him.

She let out a long breath. "She"—Death's name was never spoken aloud, not if you were a Power too and knew who she really was—"wants you back right away. Urgent business."

That was a risk; Death would see straight through it and want to know what was going on, but there was no alternative, not when the seeing man lay crumpled on the ground like he already belonged to the Power at the top of the food chain. And she could always say she'd only been doing as Death herself had commanded; not even any arguments, Death had said.

Pestilence considered her for a moment, then nodded and left. War—for of course she was—knelt at the side of the man who could see her. Bruises had blossomed over his face, and likely his body as well. Blood seeped from his nose, one ear, and through a patch on the side of his shirt.

Discombobulated. She'd never felt it before, and she waved her hands ineffectually over the man, biting her lip in frustration at her complete inability to do anything. She did arguments, disagreements, fights, conflicts, war. She could start them or stop them with the flick of an eyelid, but she'd never before been forced to pause and really give thought to the injuries they created.

"A hospital," she muttered, hoisting the man into her arms. "You need a doctor."

⌇⌇⌇

The first thing Rordan saw when he awoke was Jimmy, jaw twitching as though he hadn't decided yet between being furious and sympathetic. It took a moment longer to realise that he was in a hospital bed, surrounded by medical paraphernalia that beeped and chirped and gurgled at him, and that he was plugged in to both oxygen and an IV drip.

"What happened?" Jimmy clearly hadn't made up his mind altogether, but for now at least it looked like sympathy may win out.

"Don't remember," Rordan mumbled, and winced as the subtle movement brought to life a litany of articulate complaints from every muscle group he possessed.

Jimmy's jaw worked again, this time as though hiding a knife-edged smile.

Bastard. He knows I'm hurting. "How long have I been out?"

Jimmy's expression changed, and some of the coldness fled. "Couple of days. Had to get Susie to write your story for you."

"A couple of *days*?" Hell. *Hell.* Memories flooded back. Five Powers, three who'd been reported dead decades ago. Three reported dead, and the fourth… Everyone was content to believe there'd only ever been twelve Powers. But now he knew better; he'd seen the thirteenth.

Two days. What could they have done in two days? He didn't want to know. Only he had to, because no one else did. Ignoring his body's protests, he shoved back the covers and swung his legs over the side of the bed.

"Whoa! Hey! What do you think you're doing?" Jimmy leapt back, alarmed.

"I'm getting up. I have work to do."

"Are you insane? Look at you!"

Rordan glanced down, stomach churning as he saw the bruising over his belly and hips and thighs, bright yellow and black and red and blue, like something off an angry artist's palette. He blinked, then shook his head. "Doesn't matter. I have to stop her."

"Her who?" Jimmy's finger hovered over the call button.

"Thirteen," he said quietly. "You know the oldest sources say thirteen Powers, not twelve."

Jimmy's eyes tightened and his lips pinched. He pressed the call button. "No. There were never thirteen." The light above the doorway lit up. "Death is not a Power. Death is mindless, impersonal, and a cold, hard, fact of life."

Rordan stared pleadingly at the door. "Jimmy, please. I have to go."

"Go where?" A nurse bustled into the room, tutting as she saw him on his feet. "Right, you just lay back down, we'll have you sorted in no time." Brushing his protests aside, she bullied him back into bed—and he was ashamed to realise that, after standing for barely a minute or two, he was glad to let her. He swallowed and closed his eyes, and willed his screaming muscles to stop. He'd sneak out later, when Jimmy was gone.

<hr>

Avoid Her, that was the main thing to do right now. No doubt that prat Pollution had ratted her out to Death right away, which meant she needed to keep a low profile for the next little while. Luckily, that was exactly what

Death had ordered, so she could always claim absolute innocence if her scarcity was noted. She hadn't survived this long without an intimate understanding of strategy—something which, she had to admit, was kind of a given bonus when your name was War.

So, she'd lie low for a while. And if she happened to spend that time poking around the apartment of the man who saw her, what was that? She was assessing a risk, that was all. Trying to decide how much damage had been done when she'd saved him.

Damage to the campaign, that was, of course.

Definitely not damage to the very careful walls she'd spent the last few centuries constructing.

Carefully, Rordan examined himself for injuries. He still ached, but not so badly as he had done, and he found he could sit up without getting dizzy this time.

Was there any point, though? Was there anything to go out *to*, anything he could actually *do*? Or was he better off just lying here, ignoring it all, hoping it would go away?

Deep inside, the instinct that had made him a good reporter in the first place told him he had to move. The story was paramount, after all.

Carefully, he stripped the needles from his veins, sealing the tape back over the pricks of blood that welled. He cast around for his clothing, found his jacket and jeans but no shirt or underwear. It'd have to do.

Behind his curtain he shimmied into his clothing, rough against his still-raw skin, then headed out into the corridor. It was only when he saw a nurse rushing in the other direction that he realised his feet were cold because he had no shoes.

He wound his way through the corridors with less idea where he was going than energy to go, and as his chest heaved and his lungs strained, he realised that that was even less than he'd thought. Perhaps he'd need to have a break, risk sitting down for a moment to catch his breath.

Maybe around the next corner. Just one more. One more wouldn't kill him.

A security guard. The reporter's voice in the back of his head niggled at him, whispering ideas. He tilted his head and stared at the door behind the guard. A guard in a hospital. Hmm. It might be. It wasn't beyond the realms of possibility. He was in the right hospital, after all.

He moved towards the guard, wondering if this constituted a new low in his flagrant disregard for his own safety, or if perhaps this was his subconscious's way of trying to land him back in bed.

The guard ignored him.

A set up, then? And if he touched the swinging door, alarms would sound, the guard would wrestle him to the ground?

Holding his breath, he took a step closer, fingers outstretched.

Still the guard ignored him.

Heart pounding like he'd just survived a beating, been unconscious in bed for two, maybe three days, and was now contemplating breaking into the hospital room of the nearly-dead, last-remaining Power of the world, Rordan touched the door.

Nothing.

He blinked once for surprise, once for suspicion, then remembered the sacred motto of good journalism: Never look the gift horse in its mouth.

He opened the door, and looked into the face of the last remaining Power.

For a moment Rordan's breath caught, but then he remembered the guard and slipped into Simon Baker's isolation room, patting down his pockets instinctively for a pen and pad of paper.

Finding neither, he grasped with fists at empty air a few times, ran his hands over his head, licked his lips, and eventually sat down in the chair by Mr Baker's bed.

"Mr Baker?" he ventured, softly at first, a murmur like the falling of perfect snowflakes, then again louder.

"Mr Baker? I know you're not very well, and dying, but they say that the unconscious can hear sometimes still, and I need to know. Is it true? Are you really the last Power? Or are there more? And how can we have forgotten, if there are more? What are they planning? Why is it happening? Please, just tell me why."

The man whose other name was Memory lay still.

Rordan sank his face into his hands, pressing back the wetness that rose along with despair in his throat. This was it. He had the story—five Powers kill off the others, declare Armageddon, world to end shortly—but no real proof, nothing he could print, and worst of all, no way to stop it happening.

The world was too caught up in *now* to care. They'd forgotten that Mr Baker had had a son, had once been an ordinary green grocer, had had a wife, and a home, just like them, though granted that was a secret even the history books had been reluctant to give up. They'd forgotten that the Powers held the balance, kept the peace, made life worth living. They'd forgotten—hell, they'd forgotten that there were still five more Powers out there, roaming the world, now without their equals as humanity fought to strip the supernatural away and leave only the finite, the explicable, the measurable.

"They've forgotten," he muttered to himself. "They've forgotten."

"Remind them."

He opened his eyes and was for the first and last time in his life pinned by the gaze of Memory, silver eyes heavy with the weight of every year behind them.

"How?" he whispered.

Simon Baker, called Memory, smiled. "A new Memory is born. The world will remember."

Rordan leaned closer, fingers knotted between his knees.

A new Memory? Rordan supposed that if Simon Baker had once been human, a new Memory wasn't outside possibility.

His pulse sped. "But how? How do I find them?"

The smile of the man who used to be Memory widened. "The same way we always do: one Power to another."

A torrent broke over his head, memories crashing down, knowledge of the years and decades and centuries and millennia, filling all the crevices in his heart that he'd known were there, but had forgotten about, and he knew, he remembered—he remembered.

<hr>

War jerked mid-stride as though struck by an electric current. "No," she whispered. "No, we made sure it wasn't possible." And yet, there it was: somewhere, a new Power was being born. Her boss would not be happy.

Oh, it wouldn't utterly decimate their plans or anything; nothing so dramatic as that. They'd been waiting decades, centuries; one last Power to remove was no particular problem. But still. They'd been close, so close, and She would be… displeased.

War shivered at the idea of having that displeasure focused on her. Perhaps best to avoid Her for a bit, at least until the identity of this new Power was made known.

Who would it be? she wondered. Which Power had managed to hang on long enough, had managed to find someone worthy of assuming the mantle?

But there was only one option, really, only one Power still clinging by a thread to life in a palliative care bed in the hospital.

Her heart pounded; she'd dropped *him* there, the one who could see. He would make a perfect Power.

Death, she swore in her head. *Don't let him be Peace. Whatever else has happened, just don't let him become Peace.*

It was Memory, of course, who lay bedridden but not yet dead; but if the man who saw her became Peace, she didn't think the world would survive her outrage, because War was bound to battle Peace, from now until eternity.

If he became Memory, though…

She rounded the corner, walking quickly, contemplating the characteristics necessary for a man to truly see a woman called War.

<p style="text-align: center">~~~~~~</p>

Rordan wandered down the snowy street, mind ablaze with the memories of all that had ever happened in that place. He looked at a cobblestone and saw the countless feet that had trod it, the road makers who laid it, the man who shaped and fashioned it, the transporters, the miners, the geological processes that formed it.

His gaze settled on a woman, and he reeled as he saw her life history before his eyes, superimposed over reality like a screen erected over her head. He smiled. He had all the stories he could ever need now, and so much more.

He turned, and there was a woman with blazing red hair, eyes of fire, and skin of burnished copper that glowed in the light. And Memory, once called Rordan Arata, walked towards the Power named War, and smiled.

Her breath caught as he approached, and he wondered what she saw in his eyes. "Hello."

She nodded, slow and cautious, as one might before a mighty lion. "A new Power has been born."

Rordan's lips quirked in a smile. "So it seems."

Her gaze bore through him. "You saw me. How did you do that?"

Memory held out his arms and grinned. "I'm a Power."

War shook her head, biting her lip, eyes still clouded by—something. "You saw me before you were a Power. You *saw* me."

Oh. He knew what it was to be ignored, to been seen only for your role in life and nothing more. He couldn't remember the last time someone had known his favourite colour. There was no one alive who knew how he liked his coffee in the morning.

Memory reached over and took the hand of War. "Has anyone ever told you that you're beautiful?"

Her lips quirked and some of the clouds lifted. "Frequently. Usually right before beating in the heads of the ten other men in the room who are saying it."

Memory grinned with all the good humour of knowing not only the horrible things of history, but also the wonderful. "No men here, love. Only Powers."

"Yes," War said, folding her arms and pursing her lips to hide the birth of a smile. "You keep saying that."

All at once Memory grabbed her hands and it was her turn to be breathless, held by the years of his gaze. And yet, she realised, it was not their weight that held her. She'd seen that weight before, in the eyes of the last Memory, and the Memory before that.

No. The weight was not what held her.

"I think," Memory said slowly, "that being in love with War is a very dangerous thing to be."

Her pulse stammered.

"I also think," he continued, "that if anyone were to do it, Memory would be the safest. Surely..." He squeezed her fingers bloodless, eyes wide like he was the one drowning, not the one sweeping her away. "Surely, with what I remember, with everything I know..." He licked his lips.

"Darling," she said softly, detangling her hands from his. "Loving me will never be safe. I'm War. I'm conflict, and fighting, and people at odds, and crossed priorities, opposing interests, and—"

He stopped her mouth with a kiss, and the fire of ten thousand years of knowing how to kiss *exceptionally well* engulfed her.

"I don't care," he whispered against her skin. "I don't care at all."

She wrapped her arms around him and held him tight. "Perhaps," she whispered in his ear. "Perhaps there is a way."

Her stomach roiled and her palms broke out in a sweat. Could she tell him? Could she really deliver him the secret on a platter along with her head? Reveal to him the only thing she wanted more than life itself, the one thing that would stop her in her tracks every single time?

He rubbed his hands over her shoulders, down her back, around her waist and back up, up, and she shivered.

"Why would you love War?" she breathed.

She felt him smile against her cheek.

"Because I saw you," he said. "And you are human too."

War melted against Memory's shoulder. She didn't need to tell him the secret. He already knew.

THE MAKING OF
THE POWERS THAT BE

I think it's possible that this story wins the prize for taking me the longest to write. There were several years between the conception of this world and the actual completion of this story.

It's also the story with the most moving parts in its conception. Usually, for me, a story is the result of either a single prompt or concept or idea, or perhaps two-to-three colliding together.

The Powers That Be had at least four.

So, the first piece of the puzzle. Sometime early in 2010, I think I'd watched the Will Smith movie *Hancock* with my husband, and something about one of the scenes, where the super-powered humans are battling through the air, struck me. I wanted to write that.

It turned into a world where the Powers had to balance each other at all times, and for far, far too long I was stuck on the question of how many Powers to make, and who should be which one's opposites. Which leads us to puzzle piece number two, which is that I wanted to play with the inter-action between death and memory, something primarily visible in the flash fic piece *Forget* (Inklet #39), the first completed story in the Powers world.

So: I knew I had these Powers. I knew I wanted to play with the idea of death and memory, primarily in this context by setting it up so the opposite of Death wasn't Life, but rather Mem-ory itself. Then, to complicate things even further, we had puzzle piece three: an anthology call around about the time I started writing *The Powers That Be* for stories about either the Apocalypse, or the Four Horsemen of the Apocalypse, or maybe both—I forget exactly.

Puzzle piece four was that around about the same time I'd been discussing this connection between death and memory with a university professor of mine (during my teaching diploma; he had a high school student—he taught a few high school classes and a few university classes, however that worked—developing a project around the death/memory idea), I'd also read Terry Pratchett and Neil Gaiman's *Good Omens* for the first time.

It was delightful, and funny, and so very, very human, and I loved it—and it heavily influenced my idea of Horsemen and what they could be.

Like I said, this story took me forever to write—a process of I think about six or seven years of trying to figure out what on earth it was that I was trying to say, and how long this story needed to be to say it.

So this, the result, is apparently what happens when you pour *Good Omens* and the Four Horsemen of the Apocalypse and the idea of Death vs Memory and *Hancock* into a six-year-long blender and hit 'Go'.

This is why, when people ask authors where they get their ideas from, they tend to fudge the answer—because the real answer is this:

Ideas come from nowhere, and ideas come from everywhere. There's basically no in-between.

DOWNLOAD YOUR FREE EBOOK

When you buy a print book from Inkprint Press, we like to say THANK YOU by offering you the ebook for free!

Please head to www.inkprintpress.com/inklets/26/ and the use the coupon INKLET26 to get your copy of this Inklet in epub AND mobi today!
(Coupon will only work once.)

Read more by Amy Laurens!

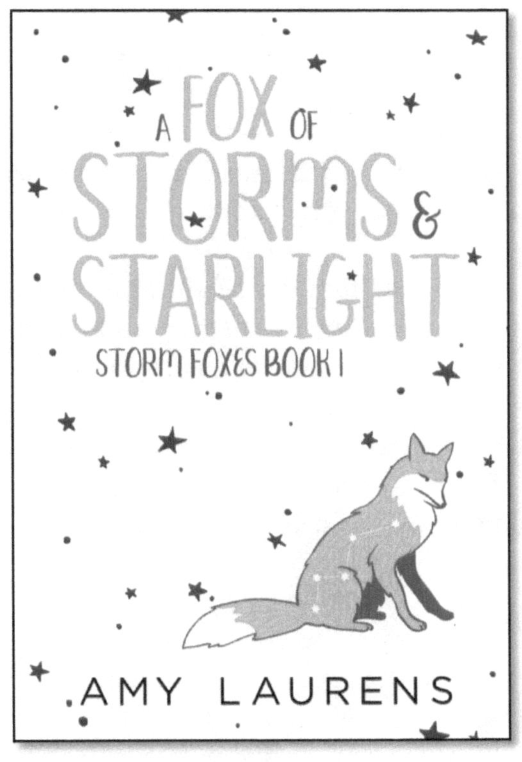

A FOX OF STORMS AND STARLIGHT

CHAPTER ONE

SIX YEARS AGO, I SAVED A FOX IN THE bush. It was only because my dog died. At the time, it felt like a pretty crappy bargain.

It was the first day of autumn—not by the calendar, but by the fresh bite in the morning air, the golden quality of the light as it lit the main road through town in the mid afternoon.

Sailor was a big, black shaggy thing, something like a Newfoundland, a lively shadow in the golden light, and I was eleven.

I'm sorry to be starting any story this way, but the fact of the matter is, this where it all began.

I'll spare you the awful details. Enough to say that Sailor had got out of the yard somehow, and had been hit by a truck careening down the highway that split our tiny town in two as it blatantly ignored the speed limit.

I saw it happen.

And although I cradled him in my lap as the smell of burnt-out brakes and hot asphalt and turning leaves filled my nose, his giant, furry black head all of him I could fit, there was nothing I could do.

There was nothing anyone could do.

I knew that, but it didn't stop the knot of frustration and guilt in my chest, or the taste of bile in the back of my throat every time I closed my eyes and saw the truck hitting him, again and again and again.

It took years for that vision to fade.

But that evening, only a few hours after it had happened, everything still felt fresh, and raw.

Sunny, my sister, was only nine at the time. She cried for hours, just sobbing like she'd never breathe right again.

I'd cried a little, at the scene with Sailor's head lying in my lap as his big, brown eye stared up at nothing.

It had been mercifully fast, there was that.

And the driver had copped a massive fine—speeding, reckless driving, I think they even defected his truck—and came to visit us later, a big, pot-bellied man standing on our front verandah, shuffling his royal blue cap round and round and round in his hands as he apologised.

But that evening, with Sunny sobbing her heart out on the couch in the living room and Mum and Dad trying desperately to console her as dinner burned on the stove, I couldn't cry, even though the acrid scent of burning soy sauce, scorching brown sugar and smoking rice wine from the marinade prickled the back of my throat and the corners of my eyes.

I was the eldest, and I had to be responsible.

Possibly, if I'd been just a little more responsible, Sailor wouldn't have died.

So I slipped out the glass slider from the family room to the deck while Sunny cried, glancing up at the two storeys of our moody grey house behind me before jumping heavily down the three steps from the rail-less deck to the lawn, and set out for the gate in the back fence.

I couldn't cry, and I didn't want to add anything to an already chaotic and stressful situation inside—but I couldn't stay there, either.

In the gaps between the gum trees to the west, the sky tinged to red and gold at the horizon, the sun sinking slowly into oblivion. I'm pretty sure I didn't know the word oblivion back then, but I knew what it meant, how it felt—and I craved it, desperately.

Anything would be better than the gaping hole in my chest.

And so, because I didn't know where to find it or how to get there, I stalked through the bush, pushing myself until I breathed hard and my lungs ached and sweat ringed me, chasing the way that hard exercise elevated me over my constantly looping thoughts.

Directly above, dark, heavy clouds obscured the sky, and the air was thick, heavy, humid.

Beneath the smell of dry gum leaves and even drier dirt, I could catch a hint of ozone, and occasionally the wind turned cool for a breath as it gusted against my skin, promising a late evening storm.

I walked harder, faster, outrunning the video looping in my mind of the truck's impact.

When the first drops of rain spat at me from out of the sky, I barely noticed. My skin was filmed with sweat, slick and salty, and the peppering of rainwater barely added to it.

That was at first.

But within minutes, it became clear that those first pattering spits had been the early foreshadowing of a storm darker and more intense than any I remembered.

Thunder rolled across the sky, distant and grumbling at first, a lazy background chorus to the rhythmic melody of the rain as it splattered down on grey-green leaves and red-tinged twigs, turning the silvered bark of an old, dead gum to deep grey and making the spiky, tussocky grass seem oddly luminescent in the dying light.

I stood under a grey gum with stains down its trunk that the rain was turning orange, arms wrapped around myself, shivering hard—and for the briefest instant, thought about not going home.

Mum and Dad would pitch a fit.

And I had to be responsible.

I turned, dark t-shirt plastered to my skin, dark hair sticking to my face and clinging to my neck, and began trudging my way back. The storm closed over properly, clouds rolling over the horizon and cutting off the thin scythe of blood-coloured sky, making the bush dark and unwelcoming in the premature night.

Lightning flashed.

Thunder cracked hot on its heels.

I jumped—and stared hard at the gap between two ghost-barked trees, where for a second, I was sure I'd seen a pair of eyes.

Nothing moved.

Nothing except the drenching rain, anyway, weighing down the branches that tossed fitfully in the wind.

The smell of wet dirt and soaked bark rose around me, undercut by eucalypt and ozone.

If anything had the power to wash away the hurt inside me, this storm was it. I tipped my face to the sky, imagining the rain washing over me had the ability to wash me inside as well, and the raindrops splattered hard on my face.

More lightning. More thunder, cracking over top of the constant hiss of the falling rain.

And in the distance, something eerie, lifting the hairs on the back of my neck: a strange kind of high-pitched howl, a cry that rang with moonlight and distance, cutting straight through the noise of the storm.

Bolts of lightning streaked across the sky—one—two—three in the space of half a second, followed immediately by a growling crack of thunder so immense it vibrated in my chest. I ducked instinctively.

There, in the corner of my eye…

I froze, crouched with my arms over my head.

The strange cries came again—and they were closer.

I stared hard at the place, low to the ground, where I was sure I'd seen something small, maybe the size of a cat.

Flash. Growl.

Rain spitting down.

There. Right there. A small animal, pointy ears, light coloured chin and throat…

The strange, eerie cries came a third time, and my heart pounded fiercely. Whatever was making the noise, it was close. Really close.

The little creature across from me reacted too, flattening itself to the ground.

My jaw twitched.

My heart pounded.

My fingertips bit into my upper arms.

Stay? Go?

Run? Freeze?

The hairs on my neck prickled again and goosebumps broke out all over me.

Cold dread formed a knot in my stomach.

Something was coming.

Something worse than the storm.

I had to get home.

I made it halfway to standing—and a series of strange, awful noises made me freeze again. They were sharp, clacking, squealing sounds, like someone knocking two echoing stones against each other, interspersed with high-pitched yowling…

And the creature in the darkness screamed.

I threw my back against the gumtree behind me, pressing hard against it. My heart hammered.

I peered back and forth in the dark, eyes wide.

Rain drenched down, but my throat was dry.

My pulse pounded faster.

The little creature screamed again—and as lightning flashed, I saw it on its back, legs slashing wildly at the air as something attacked.

The awful, clicking-yowling noises grew louder.

I slapped my hands over my ears, gasping. Water ran down my face, getting into my mouth, my eyes.

It was hurting.

Whatever the small thing was, it was getting hurt, and I'd seen enough animals hurting today.

Something in my chest snapped.

I flung myself across the ground, leaping a couple of tussocks and a fallen branch before I crashed to my knees.

I crawled closer, desperate, gasping for air through the heavy curtains of rain.

I couldn't see it. Where?

Somewhere here, near the base of that tree…

The yowling screeched right next to my ear. I cowered against the ground, spiky grass pricking my face, wet-earth smell smothering me—but now, there was a strange mustiness too, a cousin to wet-dog smell.

At the next flash of lightning, I saw it.

The creature was a fox—and something barely visible was attacking it, only the gleam of eye or flicker of teeth visible in the gloom.

But the damage was real enough.

The little fox's side had been opened right up, and in the bright, stark flashes of heavenly electricity, the blood was dark, thinned by the constant rain.

No.

No more animals were going to die today.

Not when this time, I could do something about it.

I snatched at a branch on the ground that turned out to be more of a twig, and launched myself toward the creature.

I had no idea what was attacking it, but I screamed and waved my handful of twiggy leaves anyway, batting them in the air over the fox like I knew what I was doing.

The horrible clacking cries ceased.

With one long, low rumble, the rain began to ebb.

Still gasping for air, pulse galloping in my throat, I sat next to the fox and shifted it carefully into my lap, realising as I tasted salt that I was crying.

I huddled over, trying to shelter the poor creature from the slackening rain, running my fingers over its wiry cheek— over and over and over and over.

"Please," I sobbed, throat tight and aching, chest constricted. "Please. Please don't die. Please."

Another gust of cool air washed over the clearing, taking the last of the rain with it—and lifting the goosebumps on my arms again.

I shivered, drawing the fox close, like it was a stuffed animal I could hug for comfort—its comfort or mine, I couldn't say.

"Please. Please don't die. Please."

Something shifted in my lap.

Around us, the world stilled, dazed from the storm, but also something more, something watching, something waiting, as the bush held its collective breath.

The only sound was the occasional drip of rainwater from the gum leaves onto a fallen log—no insects, no wind, no rustling of leaves. Just... stillness.

And the fox, who shivered in my lap.

The clouds tore open, revealing a ragged triangle of stars that glittered in the fox's eye as it blinked open and stared up at me.

My chest snagged.

My throat ached from crying, and a headache was forming in the back of my head. But the fox blinked up at me—alive.

I ran a finger down it again, from nose to cheek to ear to shoulder, all the way down its side to its thick, bushy tail—and the wound in its side began to close.

Laboriously, it hauled itself to its front legs.

I tried to stop it—"No, it's okay, you can stay here, I'll look after you"—but it lifted its top lip to show half-hearted teeth, and staggered away.

As it did, I thought perhaps its fur began to shrink. And suddenly, it looked larger in the night—as large as a dog, as large as Sailor…

But I blinked, and it was just a trick of the light, because the creature that darted away into the bushes like nothing was wrong at all was clearly a fox, the size of a large cat or maybe a small beagle, and nothing more.

And if something screamed in the night not long afterward, and the cry sounded horribly, horribly human?

Well. I was halfway back toward home again by then, and I pressed my fingertips to my lower eyelids and prayed my parents wouldn't murder me for getting home so late.

Keep reading! Head to
amylaurens.com/books/
storm-foxes/
to buy your copy now!

ABOUT THE AUTHOR

AMY LAURENS is an Australian author of fantasy fiction for all ages.

In addition to the *Inklet* short stories, Amy has also written the award-winning portal-fantasy *Sanctuary* series about Edge, a 13-year-old girl forced to move to a small country town because of witness protection (the first book is *Where Shadows Rise*), the humorous fantasy *Kaditeo* series, following newly-graduated Evil Overlord Mercury as she attempts to acquire a castle, the forthcoming young adult series *Storm Foxes*, about love and magic and mental health, and a whole host of non-fiction.

INKLETS

Collect them all! Released on the 1st and 15th of each month.

Welcome to Dark Dale
LIANA BROOKS

When War Came to Town
A Powers Story
AMY LAURENS

Not Fantasy
AMY LAURENS

Courting the Winter Prince
LIANA BROOKS

At the Home of the Winter King
A Storm Foxes Story
AMY LAURENS

With This Ring
AMY LAURENS

Venus &
Seven Reasons I Said No
LIANA BROOKS

Oath Keeper
AMY LAURENS

Forget
A Powers Story
AMY LAURENS

INKLET #040
Not Quite Cinderella
LIANA BROOKS

INKLET #041
ONE BAD MAN
AMY LAURENS

DOUBLE ISSUE
INKLET #042
The Claustrophobia Of Loneliness &
Adam, Be A Star
AMY LAURENS

INKLET #043
The Artist as a Young Girl
LIANA BROOKS

INKLET #044
CONFESSIONS
AMY LAURENS

INKLET #045
But For Snow
A Kaditeos Story
AMY LAURENS

INKLET #046
The Boy Named NO
LIANA BROOKS

INKLET #047
Anamata
AMY LAURENS

INKLET #048
A Wolf FOR Christmas
AMY LAURENS

www.ingramcontent.com/pod-product-compliance
Lightning Source LLC
Chambersburg PA
CBHW031034190726
48286CB00003BA/1165